FLUFFY & FRECKLES

THE PUPPY PLACE

Don't miss any of these other stories by Ellen Miles!

FLUFFY & FRECKLES

ELLEN MILES

SCHOLASTIC INC.

For Steve and the Rainbow Elves sugaring crew

CHAPTER ONE

Charles leaned against a tree, panting. "How much farther, Dad?" he asked.

Dad laughed. "Almost there," he said. "I know, it's tough going with all this snow."

Charles bent down to scoop up a handful of the clean, fresh white snow. He bit into it, letting the cold flakes fill his mouth and melt into a sip of water. "You didn't tell me we were going on a huge hike."

His father laughed again. "It only feels huge the first time. You'll get used to it. And it'll be worth it, you'll see." He ruffled Charles's hair. "I'm really glad you came with me, sport. We're going to have a lot of fun, and I know Steve will be happy for the help. Plus, we'll be here for Steve's annual Spring Fling Wing-Ding."

"His what?" Charles asked.

"It's a big open house party Steve throws every year, to celebrate maple sugaring time and the end of winter," Dad explained. "It's always a blast." He started off again, and Charles followed him, plodding along on his snowshoes.

It was spring break time, and Charles Peterson and his dad were on a special father-son trip together. Yesterday, the two of them had driven for hours to get to Vermont, where an old college friend of Dad's lived. Charles had heard a lot about Steve, and he had even met him when Steve had come to visit one time, back when Charles was only a little kid. But he had never been to Steve's place in Vermont.

On the way up, Dad had told Charles how Steve

lived all by himself, way back in the woods, in a tiny cabin. He didn't even have a driveway—at least, not in winter. As soon as the snow began to pile up, he skied or snowshoed his way home whenever he went anywhere, parking his truck at the end of a trail through the woods. Steve made his living as a carpenter, but in late winter and early spring he spent his time sugaring—making maple syrup from the trees that surrounded his cabin.

"It must be about ten years since I've come up here to help at sugaring time," Dad was saying now, as he and Charles slogged their way up the snowy trail. "But I'm sure nothing has changed. Steve still makes his syrup the old-fashioned way, all by hand. It's a lot of work, and he can always use help."

Charles didn't know much about making maple syrup, even though Dad had tried to explain it during their drive. He'd been too sleepy to pay attention to the details, but he knew the basics: at the end of winter, the sap in maple trees starts to rise. If you collect it and boil it down, you get maple syrup. Charles loved maple syrup. What was better than a plate of pancakes drowning in a golden-brown puddle of sweetness? That was exactly what they'd had for breakfast that morning at the inn where they were staying. Charles's stomach rumbled just thinking about those pancakes. With all this hiking, his breakfast had already worn off, and his tummy was empty.

"I'm hungry, Dad," he said.

"We're almost there," Dad said. "Steve promised he would have some lunch ready for us."

"I didn't think it was going to be so snowy," Charles said as he trudged through the soft, wet drifts. They were following Steve's well-packed snowshoe trail, but Charles still punched through, his whole snowshoe pushing down past the top layer of snow until he was in up to his knees on every third or fourth step. Each time, it was a struggle to pull his snowshoes back out. He could feel the cold wetness soaking through his boots and into his socks.

"I didn't, either," Dad admitted. "Steve told me they'd gotten a lot of snow this year, but I figured most of it would be melted away by now, the way it is at home. I always forget how much colder it is up here, and how much more snow they get. Even at this time of year. Steve says there's always at least one big storm in March." He stopped to catch his breath. "But look, isn't it beautiful?" He held out his arms and gazed all around. "The bare trees, the shining snow, the bright blue sky, those puffy white clouds . . . and it's so quiet! This is how I always remember Steve's woods."

Charles looked around. Dad was right, it was beautiful. He liked the feeling of the cold snow beneath him and the warm sun above. "Is that a sap bucket?" he said. "We must be getting closer." He pointed to a big, gnarled tree just off the path. Hanging from it was a silver bucket with a lid.

"The welcome tree!" Dad said. "This is always the first one Steve taps." He showed Charles where a metal spout had been pushed into a small hole drilled into the tree. The bucket was hanging from the spout. "Hear that?"

"What?" Charles asked.

Dad put his fingers to his lips. "Listen," he said.

Then Charles heard it. *Plink, plink, plink.* Droplets of sap were falling out of the spout and into the bucket. He grinned up at Dad.

Dad smiled back. "That is the true sound of spring," he said. He slid back the bucket's lid to look inside. "Only an inch or two of sap in there," he said. "Steve must have already emptied this one earlier this morning."

"Is the sap sweet?" Charles asked. His mouth was dry and he needed a drink.

"Want to taste for yourself?" Dad reached into the bucket and scooped up a handful of sap for Charles to slurp.

The sap was cold. At first, Charles was disappointed because it tasted more like water than syrup, but then it hit his tongue with just a hint of sweetness. He smiled up at Dad. "Yum," he said, putting his own hand in for another scoop.

"We can fill our water bottles later," Dad said, scooping up a handful for himself. "I remember now, how we used to always drink the sap while we were working out here. Steve says it's a spring tonic, really good for you."

"That's what Steve says, is it?" Charles whirled around to see who was talking. A tall, thin man with long gray hair tied back in a ponytail stood smiling at them, hands on hips.

"Steve!" said Dad. He stepped over to throw his arms around his friend. Steve gave him a big bear hug in return. "How'd you sneak up on us?"

"I'm like a cat," Steve said, smiling. "Welcome! I thought you'd never make it, but here you are. And here's Charles, all grown up." He stuck out his hand and Charles shook it. "Last time I saw you, you were no bigger than a duckling."

Charles laughed. He knew he'd been about as big as his younger brother, the Bean, was now, but it was still funny to be compared to a duckling.

"How's Betsy? And Lizzie?" Steve asked.

Betsy was Charles's mom, and Lizzie was his older sister.

"They're great," said Dad. "Betsy's working on a big newspaper story about our town's plan to become more energy efficient. And Lizzie—well, Lizzie's always busy with something. Usually something to do with dogs. These days she's trying to teach our puppy, Buddy, how to dance, I think."

Steve threw back his head and guffawed. "Dancing dogs! What's next? And are you still taking in all the little puppies of the world?"

Dad laughed. "Well, we are still fostering puppies, but mostly one at a time."

"Buddy was one of our foster puppies," Charles told Steve. Charles was usually shy with new grown-ups, but Steve was so friendly. "He's the only one we kept forever."

"He must be the best one then," said Steve.

"He is!" Charles said, thinking of his sweet brown puppy with the heart-shaped white spot on his chest. It would be so much fun to have Buddy along, but Lizzie had refused to let Charles and Dad take him. Charles felt his heart swell the way it always did when he thought of Buddy. His fingers itched to pet Buddy's soft, warm tummy and ruffle his silky ears.

Steve and Dad were still talking. "And the little one?" Steve asked. "Adam, right?"

"We still call him the Bean," Dad said, "the way we did when he was just a baby and looked like a little lima bean when he was sleeping. He's fine, too. Always getting into mischief."

"Excellent," Steve said, clapping Dad on the shoulder. "Glad to hear that the family is thriving. I must say it's great to have you here, old friend. Are you two ready to haul some sap?" Steve pointed to a pair of big blue plastic buckets he'd set down in the snow. "The way it works is, we empty the smaller metal buckets into these bigger buckets. Then we haul the big buckets to an even bigger tank, just over the hill there, and dump them in." He held up both arms in a muscleman pose. "It's hard work, but it'll make you strong."

"How often do you have to do it?" Charles asked.

"Every day, as long as the sap is running," said Steve. "And whether the sap runs or not depends on the weather. I hear we've got a great streak coming up right now, with the nights under freezing and the days sunny and warm. That's what the trees love most." He gave the big tree next to them an affectionate slap. "Don't you, pal?" he asked.

Charles smiled. Steve was what Mom would call a "real character." Who talked to trees? Someone who lived among them, Charles guessed. Why shouldn't Steve make friends with his neighbors, even if they weren't people?

Charles and Dad helped Steve empty a few buckets on their way to the sugarhouse, pouring the crystal-clear sap into the big blue buckets and then hanging the silver buckets back onto their taps. Charles spilled a little sap onto the snow while he was lifting a full bucket off its tap, but Steve just smiled. "It happens," he said. "Hey, want to see something? Check out these animal tracks going across the snow." He knelt down to point out a trail of little paw prints. "I'm thinking it's probably a fox," Steve said. "I've seen these tracks all around my cabin lately."

"A fox?" Charles asked. "Really? They look like puppy tracks to me."

CHAPTER TWO

Steve sat back on his haunches and looked up at Charles. "Puppy tracks?"

Charles nodded. "They look exactly like the tracks my puppy, Buddy, makes after a snowstorm."

"Well, after all, foxes are related to dogs, aren't they?" Dad asked. "So maybe—"

Steve held up a hand. "You know, I think Charles might be right. When I look more closely, I can see that these tracks are rounder and a little bigger than fox tracks. And see how the trail meanders?" He pointed. "It wanders all over the place, here, there, and everywhere. Fox trails tend to move straight in one direction. Foxes are always on a mission."

"But what would a puppy be doing all the way out here in the woods?" Charles asked, and Steve nodded.

"Right, you wouldn't expect that," he said. "As a matter of fact, this reminds me that some of my neighbors have been talking about a young stray they've been seeing this winter. I saw my friend Adelaide at the post office the other day, and she said she thought the pup had been living in her barn for a while. Maybe he's decided to drop in on me now."

"Wow," said Charles. "But—" He spun around in a circle, almost falling over his own snowshoes. Then he threw his arms out at the endless woods. "Where would he be? He could be anywhere out here. Do you think he's okay? It's cold out, and he must be hungry. We have to try to find him and help him."

Charles saw Steve look at Dad, his eyebrows raised. Dad grinned and reached out to pat Charles on the back. "That's my boy," he told Steve. "Charles can't stand to see—or even hear about—a dog in trouble."

Steve nodded seriously. "You've got a big heart, Charles. Tell you what. We've got a few more buckets of sap to collect, and as soon as we're done we'll see if we can find that pup. Okay?"

Reluctantly, Charles nodded. He did not want to wait one minute to look for the dog, but he wasn't in charge. He followed Dad and Steve down the trail, lagging behind a bit as he watched for more puppy tracks in the snow. *There!* He stooped to take a closer look. Nope. These tracks were totally different. They were tinier, and he could see the mark of a tail that had been dragging along. Plus, these tracks led straight to a tree trunk, then disappeared as if the animal had climbed right up. *Probably a squirrel*, thought Charles.

Dad and Steve had stopped up ahead in a small grove of trees. Charles could hear them talking as they emptied buckets. He looked back at the spot where he'd first seen the puppy tracks. Maybe he could just follow the trail a little way and find out where the puppy had gone. He looked at Dad and Steve again. They picked up their blue buckets and began to hike slowly up the trail, still talking. Dad was so busy catching up with his old friend that he hadn't even noticed that Charles wasn't with them.

Charles didn't stop to think about it. He turned around on the trail and headed back the way they'd come. When he got to the place where the puppy tracks crossed, he stooped down to take a closer look. Which way was the puppy headed? He could see the shape of the puppy's paw outlined perfectly in the new snow—right down to the toe-nails. It was clear that the dog had been headed toward a cluster of pine trees off to Charles's left. He stared into the dark, thick woods. Maybe the puppy was right over there, watching him! It would only take a minute or two to check. He looked back over his shoulder at Dad and Steve; they were still hiking slowly up the trail, still talking.

Charles stepped off the snowshoe path and began to follow the tracks.

Steve was right, the trail did meander, heading this way and that. "Meander," Charles said under his breath as he followed the tracks. That was a new word for him, and it was a good one. Charles liked to put words like that into his back pocket and pull them out in the middle of a conversation. He loved seeing the look on his mom's face when he did that. The other day when Buddy was barking and running around the house, Charles had said that Buddy was being obstreperous. Mom had looked surprised, then burst out laughing.

Charles smiled, remembering. Then he realized he'd lost the trail because he wasn't paying attention. He retraced his steps and picked it up again as the tracks meandered from tree to tree. He even found a place where the puppy had peed against a tall pine. "Just like Buddy," he said aloud, thinking of the way his puppy always had to sniff every bush and tree before he picked out the one he wanted.

Thinking of Mom and Buddy made Charles miss them both. They seemed very far away right then, as he stood alone in the middle of the snowy woods. Even Dad and Steve seemed pretty far away. Charles took a deep breath, which helped to undo the sudden lump in his throat, and kept walking.

The day seemed darker when Charles entered

the piney grove where the puppy's tracks led. He had to squint to see the trail, and push heavy snow-laden branches out of his way in order to follow the tracks. Charles saw a spot where the puppy had stopped to scrape away some snow—maybe he'd smelled something interesting there—and then continued on.

The tracks kept going, and Charles kept pushing forward until he popped out into a small clearing near a stone cliff that had moss growing all over it, even now in winter. It was pretty, the way melting snow trickled down the bright green moss and made it shine.

But—Charles knelt down and looked more closely to be sure—the tracks seemed to head directly for the cliff, then disappear. A puppy couldn't walk straight up that steep rock face! Where had he gone?

As Charles knelt, he heard a tiny whimper.

Then another. He peered along the bottom of the cliff until he spotted a dark triangle where there was an opening in the rock. The tracks led right into it!

"Hello?" Charles said. He listened carefully, and heard another soft whimper in reply. Slowly, he crawled forward. "Puppy? Are you in there?" Then he stopped, frozen in his tracks, wondering all of a sudden whether Steve had been right in the first place. Maybe those tracks really had been made by a fox, and maybe the fox was holed up in this little cave, just where a fox belonged. On the one hand, Charles thought he would really love to see a fox, a flash of red fur and a long, thick tail in the middle of these snowy, piney woods. But on the other hand . . . Were foxes nice, or were they scary? Did foxes bite? What would happen if a fox suddenly ran out of that tiny dark cave, straight at Charles?

Charles stood up quickly and turned to look over his shoulder. Which way should he run if that happened? Which way was out, anyway? He could follow his own tracks, but then he'd be pushing through the trees again. There must be an easier way back to the trail.

The trail! Where were Dad and Steve? Hadn't they noticed by now that he wasn't with them? They were probably looking for him. At least, he hoped they were. He cleared his throat. "Dad?" he called, but his voice seemed very tiny. "Dad?" he called again, louder.

He heard a tiny rustle and turned around just in time to see a little brown-and-white face at the entrance to the small cave in the rocks. The face was framed with two long, floppy ears, one brown and one white with brown spots.

Definitely not a fox.

Charles's heart thumped in his chest, but he

didn't move a muscle. He didn't want to scare the puppy, who already looked frightened.

"Hi, there," he said softly.

The face disappeared.

Charles waited, staying very still.

The face popped out again. This time, the puppy tilted his head in a questioning way, just like Buddy always did.

Who are you? Should I be afraid? Yes. I think I will. Being afraid is always safer.

Again, the face disappeared.

Moving slowly, Charles squatted down. "C'mon, pal," he said softly. "You don't have to worry. I won't hurt you."

Charles thought of how Lizzie had once called him a "puppy whisperer" because he seemed to be able to connect with any puppy, no matter how scared or shy they were. Could he whisper this puppy out of its hidey-hole and into his arms? He slid a hand into the pocket of his jeans, hoping to find at least a piece of a dog biscuit to tempt the puppy with. Nothing. He tried all his pockets, but they were empty.

When he glanced back at the cave entrance, he saw that the puppy was peering out again. His face was so cute, with a big brown spot surrounding one eye and freckles of brown sprinkled all over. Charles held out his hand. "Hey, Freckles," he whispered. "Come on out. I don't have anything to give you, but I'm still a friend."

"Charles!" a shout boomed behind him.

"Dad!" Charles stood up and ran, clomping through the snow on his snowshoes, into his father's arms.

"What are you doing way back in the woods here?" Dad asked. He looked a little mad at first, but then he knelt down to give Charles a huge hug. "I thought we'd lost you."

"But now we found you," Steve said, coming up behind them.

"I followed those tracks." Charles blurted out the whole story. "It was a puppy! A brown-and-white one. He's so cute, but he's really shy. And now he won't come out!" he finished, pointing to the cave. No freckled face peered back at them. Would the grown-ups believe him?

"Nice tracking," said Steve, nodding. "But I'm not surprised that this pup is shy. He's been living on his own for a while, from what I hear. Probably half-wild by now." He dug into his jacket pocket. "Still, I bet he might be tempted by something really good to eat. And I just happen to have a leftover turkey sandwich right here."

CHAPTER THREE

Steve unfolded the white paper around the sandwich, then lifted off the top piece of bread so the turkey slices showed. "This looks like something that might tempt a hungry pup, hey?" He held it out for Charles to take. "Worth a try, anyway."

Charles peeled off a few slices of turkey, then walked closer to the little cave. "Puppy?" he called. "Freckles?"

"You've already named him?" Dad asked.

"Shhh." Charles turned around with his finger to his lips. "He's shy. He'll never come out if we keep talking."

Dad frowned. Charles knew he shouldn't have

shushed him, but he really, really wanted that dog to come out. "Sorry," he mouthed. Dad nodded and waved a hand to let Charles know it was okay. He got it—he knew how much puppies meant to Charles.

Charles squatted down, holding out a piece of turkey. He was hoping that the smell of meat would waft into the little cave. Sure enough, after a few moments he saw movement, and the little face appeared again. "Hi, pup," said Charles. "Want some?"

The puppy's nose twitched, but he didn't move.

Charles held out his hand a little closer.

"Are you sure he's friendly?" Dad asked in a low voice.

Charles waved a hand, meaning both "yes" and "be quiet!"

The face disappeared.

Charles turned around. "Dad!" he said.

"Okay, okay," said his father. "I'll be quiet." He pretended to zip his lips. "Just don't get too close until we have a better idea of what this dog is like."

Charles nodded and turned back to the cave. He waited patiently until the face reappeared. Then he pinched off a small piece of turkey and tossed it, hoping to get it closer to the puppy.

It landed a foot from the cave entrance. The puppy's nose twitched again, but he didn't step forward. Charles saw him lick his lips.

"Aha! You're hungry," said Charles softly. "I knew it." He tore off another piece and tossed it a little farther. This time it landed right in front of the puppy.

The puppy's nose twitched. He licked his lips again.

That smells so good. I'm scared to come out—but I can't resist.

He bent to gobble it up. Then he cocked his head and looked straight at Charles, as if asking for more.

"Yessss," Charles said under his breath. He tossed another piece. This time, the puppy didn't duck back into the cave. Instead, he gobbled that piece—and stepped forward to grab the first scrap of turkey that Charles had thrown, too. He tossed another piece, a little way in front of the puppy.

The puppy didn't move.

And then he did. He took one step, stretched out his skinny neck, and grabbed up the piece of meat. Then he stepped back.

Charles sighed. This was going to take forever! His legs were tired from squatting, so he stood up to give them a stretch. The puppy disappeared back into his cave.

"Let me try for a while," said Steve. Charles

handed over the turkey and went to stand by Dad while Steve squatted down.

"Steve's always had a way with animals," Dad told Charles in a low voice. "He doesn't have any pets—says he doesn't want the responsibility—but he's like you. He can't ignore an animal in need. He even helps out his farmer friends sometimes when they have a baby animal who needs extra care." Dad put a hand on Charles's shoulder. "Don't worry, we'll get the puppy out of there."

They watched as Steve tossed piece after piece of turkey toward the cave entrance. The puppy reappeared and began to snatch up the treats. Steve stayed very still, and murmured things that Charles could barely hear. "That's it" and "okay, friend" and things like that.

Soon Steve was making shorter and shorter throws, and the puppy was coming closer and closer to him. Charles held his breath. Now he could see how thin the puppy was, and how he was shivering as he stood in the snow. Was he trembling with fright or from cold? Probably both, thought Charles. His heart went out to the brave little pup who had been living on his own all winter.

What kind of dog was Freckles, anyway? Lizzie was the one who could always guess dog breeds, but Charles was pretty sure that this pup wasn't any particular breed—more like a mix of several different types. He had never seen another dog quite like Freckles—not even on Lizzie's big "Dog Breeds of the World" poster—but Charles loved the puppy's spots, his long ears, and his sweet face.

"I'm running out of turkey," Steve said, without turning his head. "But I think I can almost grab him. Be ready if he runs past me."

Charles watched closely as Steve threw one

more piece of turkey, very close to the tip of his own snowshoe. The pup slowly crept closer, stopping to eye Steve every few seconds. Then, when he bent his head to take the meat, Steve swept out a long arm and grabbed him by the scruff of the neck.

"Got him!" he said, pulling the puppy into his arms.

Charles saw the puppy squirm and wriggle, but Steve held him calmly and firmly, and soon he settled down.

"Now what?" Steve grinned up at Charles.

Charles opened his mouth—and closed it again. He hadn't really thought that far ahead. He looked at Dad. "Well, we were about due for a foster puppy, right?" he asked. It had been a while since the Petersons had helped a puppy in need.

"Whoa!" Dad held up his hands. "Hold on, there," he said. "How can we do that? We're not home, remember? We're staying at an inn. I don't think they allow pets there."

Charles looked back at the puppy, who had nestled into Steve's wool jacket. He could see, even from where he stood, that the puppy was still shivering. "But we can't leave him in the woods," he said. "Maybe we should go back home early so we can foster him there?"

Dad shook his head. "Nope. We promised Steve we'd help him with sugaring, and I'm not going to back out on that. Maybe there's an animal shelter around here that can take him."

Charles felt his heart sink. Some animal shelters were warm, welcoming places—but even so, they were not homes. Puppies needed homes, places where they could really feel safe, and loved, and cared for. Especially scared, skinny puppies who weren't used to people. Charles looked at the little face peeking out from Steve's arms.

Steve stood up, still cradling the puppy. "I guess he'll have to bunk with me for a night or two while we figure it out," he said. "I don't have much room, but at least my place stays warm, thanks to my woodstove."

Charles grinned up at him. "Really? That would be so great." He couldn't wait to get to know this puppy, to play with him, to find out where and how he liked to be petted, and what he liked to eat.

"You'll have to help out, though," Steve said. "I can't have him underfoot while I'm trying to gather sap and boil it up. This is a busy time for me."

"Of course," said Charles. He couldn't stop smiling as he followed Dad and Steve back through the pine grove and down the trail to Steve's cabin. Everything was working out perfectly.

It turned out that the cabin was very nearby, just over the hill. "That's where we boil the sap,"

Steve said, gesturing to a small shed with a metal stovepipe sticking up from its roof. "I'll show you all that later." He led them to the little log cabin behind the shed, and pushed open the door with his foot as he carried the puppy inside. "Welcome," he said as he waved Charles and Dad in.

"It's so cozy!" Charles burst out. The cabin was warm and smelled like woodsmoke. It was mainly one big room, with windows all around. There was a tiny kitchen along one wall and a big, comfy-looking couch along another. A ladder led to a sleeping loft above the couch. The other two walls were covered in bookshelves. Stacks of books filled every horizontal surface. A rocking chair sat next to a shiny blue woodstove that pumped out waves of heat. Charles could just picture Steve sitting in that chair on a quiet winter evening, reading as he rocked back and forth.

"Cozy, for sure," said Steve. "Some folks think it's awfully small, but it seems to fit me just fine."

"I like it," said Charles. But his mind was on Freckles. "Do you have something we can use to make a bed for the puppy?"

"Sure," said Steve. Why don't you grab those old towels hanging on a hook behind the door, there?" Steve was still holding Freckles in his arms, and he jutted his chin to show Charles where to go.

Charles could see that the dog's eyelids were drooping, and he could tell the exhausted puppy was about to fall asleep. He was dying to pet the dog, but first he wanted to make sure that Freckles would be comfortable. He ran for the towels. Steve told him to put them on the floor near the woodstove, "And add a couple of those pillows from the couch, too," he said. "Let's make him comfy. The poor little dude has been living rough."

While Charles set up a little bed for Freckles, Steve told Dad where to find some bowls for water and food. "I guess he'll just have to eat leftovers tonight," Steve said. "And I'm sure he'll be happy for them. I'll pick up a bag of food when I go to town for the mail tomorrow."

Steve knelt on the floor to settle Freckles onto the towels. "There you go," he said. "You rest for a while."

Charles knelt down, too. The puppy looked up at him with sad golden-brown eyes, and Charles could see that he was still trembling. "Think I can pet him?" he asked Steve.

"He still seems pretty scared," Steve said. "But if you're gentle, he might let you."

Charles reached out a hand, slowly, slowly.

Freckles drew his head back and ducked out of the way.

Charles tried not to let it hurt his feelings. "It's okay, Freckles," he said softly. "I know you're scared. But soon you'll figure out that I'm your friend." Charles hoped he was right. But meanwhile, he could see that Freckles had found the perfect, peaceful place to spend a few nights.

CHAPTER FOUR

"Dad?" Charles asked the next morning.

"That's my name," said Dad, grinning. "What's up?" He held tight to the steering wheel, yanking it this way and that as he drove up the muddy, rutted road. After another pancake breakfast at their inn, they were on their way back to Steve's sugarbush. Charles had learned that was the name of a bunch of maple trees all growing together. The sun was shining and there wasn't a single cloud in the blue, blue sky.

Charles couldn't wait to get there. He had thought about Freckles all night, wondering how to convince the adorable pup that he was a friend.

He was so eager to hug the little dog and bury his nose in his soft-looking fur. At breakfast, Charles had snuck a few pieces of sausage from his plate into a napkin, and then into his pocket. His pocket felt a bit greasy now, but it didn't matter. Charles knew that no dog could resist sausage. It might take time, but Charles was sure that he and Freckles would be pals by the end of the day.

"What's up?" Dad repeated.

"I was just wondering," Charles said, remembering the question he'd had for Dad. "Do you think Steve is lonely?"

Dad shook his head. "No, I don't. Steve has plenty of friends around here, people who really love him. He knows their kids and even their grandkids by now, since he's lived here for a long time. But he also really likes to live alone."

"Way out there at the cabin?" Charles said. "I'd be lonely *and* scared."

"There's nothing to be afraid of out in those woods," Dad said. "And I don't think Steve will ever be lonely as long as he's got his books. You know, it's like my dad used to say: 'Different people are different.' We don't all want the same things in life, and that's fine. Your mom and I couldn't wait to have kids and live in a small, friendly town. But Steve likes to live alone in the woods."

Charles nodded. He could tell that Dad was right. Steve's cabin was such a peaceful and happy place, even if it was in the middle of nowhere.

Dad was also right about something else: the hike to Steve's cabin did not seem as long on the second day. Maybe it was the magnetic pull of Freckles—Charles felt like his feet were flying along the path, clumsy snowshoes and all.

Dad knocked on Steve's door, but there was no

answer. "He must be out gathering sap," Dad said, peering into the empty cabin. "And I guess Freckles is with him."

Charles was disappointed. He couldn't wait to see Freckles. "Well, let's go find them," he said.

"Okay," said Dad. "Grab a couple of buckets and we'll follow his snowshoe tracks. The ones from today will be fresher and we'll be able to tell where he went." Sure enough, as soon as they'd climbed a hill and followed a stone wall for a while, there was Steve, his bright red wool jacket making him easy to spot. He was whistling as he dumped buckets of sap into his blue buckets, and—Charles could hardly believe his eyes— there was Freckles prancing along in Steve's footsteps, tail wagging happily. He was a different pup from the cowering, trembling stray Charles had seen last night.

"Freckles!" Charles called, dropping down onto

his knees in the snow. He flung his arms wide open. "Come here, boy!"

Steve looked up and waved, hooting a long "Helloooo!" The skinny brown-and-white pup leaned against Steve's legs and stared at Charles. Then the puppy looked up at Steve. And back at Charles.

Um, I know we've met before, but I'm still feeling shy.

"It's okay," Steve said, smiling down at him. "Charles is cool. Go check him out." He waved in Charles's direction, and after a few hesitant steps away from Steve, Freckles seemed to make up his mind.

Well, if the tall man likes you, I guess you really are okay.

Charles burst out laughing as Freckles bounded toward him, surfing through the snow like a dolphin leaping in the waves. "Good boy," he called, opening his arms even wider. He loved the way the puppy's ears flapped and bounced as he ran. His brown spots stood out against the white snow.

Charles couldn't wait to hug him, but the pup stopped short a few feet away. "Okay," Charles said. "It's a good start, anyway." He reached into his pocket, broke off a little piece of sausage, and tossed it to Freckles, who gobbled it right down.

Dad picked up a couple of blue buckets. "Let's go gather some sap, okay?" he said. "You can keep an eye on Freckles while we work."

"I hope he doesn't run away," Charles said as they got closer to Steve.

"Oh, he won't," said Steve. "This pup knows a good thing when he sees it. I could tell he really enjoyed sleeping by that woodstove and having a warm meal—even if it was only leftover beef stew."

Freckles pranced right up to Steve and leaned against him.

Yup. Life is pretty good right now.

Charles felt a twinge of envy. Freckles really seemed to like Steve. He knew it made sense, since Steve had been taking such good care of the pup, but still. Dogs always liked Charles, and Charles was proud of that.

He felt Dad's hand on his shoulder. "Patience," Dad said, with a wink.

How did Dad always seem to know exactly what Charles was thinking?

Charles smiled back at Dad. He knew he could make friends with Freckles. Dad was right, he just had to be patient. He headed to a metal bucket hanging on a nearby tree and emptied it into his bigger blue bucket. The crystal-clear sap sparkled in the sunlight as he poured.

"We'll get enough sap to start boiling today," Steve said as they trudged along the paths, lugging the heavy buckets. "I'm going to fire up the arch soon."

"The arch?" Charles asked.

"That's what we call the setup back there in the shed. There's a long metal pan that sits on top of a long iron box full of burning wood. The sap fills up the metal pan and starts to boil over that hot fire, and after a while it gets thick and sweet enough to be syrup. Then we draw it off and bottle it up."

"Cool," said Charles. He noticed that Freckles was leaning against Steve's leg again. He reached into his pocket, pulled out another little piece of sausage, and tossed it to Freckles. The puppy caught it in midair and gobbled it down.

"You'll make friends fast that way," Steve said, smiling at Charles. "Our buddy here is a hungry guy."

By the time they had finished emptying all the buckets, Charles was sore and tired. Gathering sap was hard work, especially with so much snow to wade through. Steve's paths meandered around the beautiful open woods: over hills, along stone walls, and beneath moss-covered rocky ledges. Steve had names for each of the areas within his sugarbush: the North Slope, the Old West, the Hinterlands.

Charles was sore and tired—but he was happy, too. Thanks to the sausage, Freckles was already beginning to come all the way up to him when he called. He let Charles scratch his head and pet his neck. Once, he even leaned against Charles.

Back at the sugaring shed, Steve lit a wood fire that he'd laid inside the long firebox. He turned a valve on a long pipe that came out of the tank, and sap started to fill the metal trays on top of the fire. "See, in this section of the tray the sap starts to warm up," he said, pointing. "Then it goes into this part, and really starts to boil hard. The sap has to boil a lot to make syrup, and most of it goes up in steam. It takes over forty gallons of sap to make one gallon of syrup!"

Charles sat in an old lawn chair where he would be out of the way while Dad and Steve worked at the arch. Freckles lay down next to him and let Charles pet his head. Dad split wood with a hatchet while Steve fed the fire. Soon a cloud of sweet-smelling steam was rolling off the boiling sap. "Will it be syrup soon?" Charles asked. The bright late-winter sun warmed the top of his head. Freckles was already snoozing, and Charles felt like he could fall asleep, too.

"Not for a while," Steve said. "If you want, you

can take Freckles into the cabin and give him some food. I left sandwich stuff out on the counter, too. Make yourself some lunch."

"Make us all some lunch," said Dad. "We're stuck out here minding the fire and the sap."

"Really?" Of course, Charles knew how to make a sandwich. But he'd never, like, been in charge in the kitchen. "Okay." He stood up. "C'mon, Freckles," he said, patting his thigh. Freckles jumped right up. He gave Steve one quick glance, then followed Charles to the cabin.

Charles filled Freckles's bowl with kibble, then got going on the sandwich-making. He worked happily in Steve's kitchen, with Freckles at his feet. He set out six slices of bread, spread mayo and mustard on them, added some lettuce he found in the fridge, and then carefully laid cheese and ham slices over that. Once in a while he pretended to drop a little piece of cheese, just so Freckles could hoover it up.

Finally, he cut the sandwiches in half like Mom always did and piled them on a plate. He grabbed a bag of chips from the counter and headed outside with the food, Freckles trotting at his heels. Steve was right: this dog wasn't about to run off anytime soon. Freckles really did know a good thing when he saw it.

"You're just in time," Steve called when Charles put the plate down on the old picnic table near the sugar shack. "We're about to draw off some finished syrup."

CHAPTER FIVE

Charles joined his dad and Steve by the arch. The billowing steam made a sweet cloud that fogged Charles's glasses. "See, take a look at the thermometer," said Steve. "The sap is up to a hundred eighteen degrees now, which is just about perfect."

Charles squinted at the old brass thermometer, but between his fogged-up glasses, the cloud of steam, and the tiny numbers smeared with years of woodsmoke and syrup, he couldn't make out a thing.

"Don't worry," Dad said, laughing. "I couldn't read that thermometer ten years ago, and now it's even more tarnished and worn."

Steve set a tall metal canister beneath a tap at the side of the metal pan and turned the valve so that hot, golden syrup began to run out, filling up the can.

"Wow," said Charles, watching the syrup flow. "That's enough for, like, a million pancakes."

"We'll put this into jars, and I'll send you home with some," said Steve. "You won't believe how good it is, fresh off the arch."

Charles and Dad smiled at each other. Sugaring was hard work, but it was about the most fun hard work Charles had ever done. Especially with Freckles around. He was so curious about everything; he loved to follow Steve everywhere, watching him closely. Charles had a feeling that Freckles was tired of living on his own, and ready to settle down—the question was, where? Usually, Charles and Lizzie worked hard on finding homes for the puppies their family fostered, but he didn't know anybody up in Vermont—well, except for Kit Smithers, Lizzie's favorite author. But she had already adopted one of their foster pups and wasn't looking for another dog.

Late that afternoon, when Dad and Charles were about to head back to the inn, Steve said, "I think I'd better pick you two up in my truck tomorrow morning. That dirt road is just getting muddier and bumpier these days, with the temperatures going up and down. I don't want you losing your muffler or getting stuck somewhere."

"Fine with me," said Dad, taking off his work gloves. "Are you sure you don't want to come to town tonight and let us take you out to dinner?"

Steve shook his head. "I'm not going anywhere as long as this sap is still boiling," he said. "Anyway, I'm fine here on my own. I'm used to it, you know."

Dad nodded. "We'll see you tomorrow, then."

Charles didn't want to leave Freckles. The pup was getting friendlier and friendlier as he felt safer and more comfortable in his temporary home. He'd even come up to Charles a few times, looking for a treat. He would lean against Charles's leg, gaze up at him with those golden-brown eyes, and wag his tail.

I'm beginning to trust you. And I like the way you scratch the top of my head. How do you know exactly the right place to do that? It feels so good.

"I'll see you tomorrow, pal," said Charles as he and Dad left. He gave Freckles one more of the special treats he'd bought at the general store in town. Then he gave the puppy's head one last scratch. At least Freckles was happy at the cabin, even if he couldn't come with them to their inn.

As soon as breakfast was over the next morning, Charles sat on the glassed-in sunporch of their inn, watching for Steve's truck. It was windy and cold outside, and the sky was flat white. Suddenly, it felt more like winter again. He remembered that the innkeeper had told them last night that the weather was likely to change. "What time did Steve say he'd come?" he asked Dad. Charles couldn't believe how much he missed Freckles. He had a feeling that today would be the day Freckles would be ready for some hugs, and he couldn't wait to throw his arms around the soft brown-and-white pup.

Dad sighed as he checked his watch for the tenth time. "Steve's not always too exact about timing," he said. "But he'll be here soon. He needs our help up there at the sugarbush, so I'm sure he won't forget us."

Finally, Charles saw the dark blue truck pull up

in front. "Steve's here!" he said, jumping up to run outside. Would Freckles be in the truck? Charles hoped so. Then they could share the backseat while Steve drove up the bumpy, rutted road. Maybe Charles would get that puppy hug right away.

Steve climbed out of the truck, and Freckles leapt out after him. "Freckles!" Charles cried, opening his arms. The pup came running over, wagging his tail.

Hi, friend, hi, friend!

He sniffed Charles and let him scratch his head, but when Charles tried to hug him he pulled away. Charles was disappointed but he understood. Freckles was still a little shy. "It's okay, pal," he said. "I get it. I'll be patient."

"Hop in," said Steve. "We've got one more stop to make."

Charles got into the backseat with Freckles, and Dad climbed into the front seat next to Steve. "Where are we headed?" he asked.

"To my friend Chloe's farm," Steve said. "I got word at the post office that she needs a favor from me."

"What kind of favor?" Dad asked. Charles was wondering, too.

"You'll see," said Steve, smiling a mysterious smile.

Charles sat back and let Freckles put his paws on his lap. He scratched the soft fur behind the puppy's floppy ears. Charles couldn't decide whether he liked the brown ear or the freckled ear best. Finally, he decided he liked them both: it was the mixture of the two colors that made Freckles so special.

Freckles gazed up at him with half-closed eyes, a contented look on his face.

I was okay living in the woods by myself, but I have to admit that I could get used to this petting thing. It's pretty nice.

Steve whistled as he drove along, steering the truck carefully to avoid the deepest of the muddy ruts in the road. Finally, he turned up a long drive-way, also muddy, and bumped along until he pulled to a stop in front of a big red barn. He tooted the horn a couple of times, and a woman popped out from behind the barn. She waved. "Hurray!" she called. "Just in time. Come on out back."

"Better leave Freckles in the truck," Steve said to Charles. "Chloe's got a lot of critters here and we don't know how he'd act around them."

Charles hated to leave Freckles, but he was curious about what they were doing at Chloe's farm. Did she need help fixing something? Lifting something?

Steve led them around to the back of the barn. There stood Chloe, in the middle of a fenced pen, surrounded by a crowd of big woolly sheep. She had rosy cheeks and sparkling eyes, and cradled in her arms was a tiny white lamb. It had the cutest face, and funny ears that stuck out sideways. Chloe grinned at Steve. "You sure about this? I know you're busy, too, this time of year."

Steve shrugged. "Busy, but I'm not going anywhere. And I've got some excellent helpers." He introduced Charles and his father.

Chloe nodded. "Great. You really only need to take him for a night, until I get caught up enough to take over the bottle feeding. We had seven other lambs born last night and this morning, and more to come. Lambing season! It's always hectic."

"Wait, are we taking a lamb home?" Charles asked. He stared at the tiny fluffy animal in

58

Chloe's arms. It was the most adorable thing he had ever seen. It almost seemed to be smiling back at him.

"Well, that's the plan," Steve said. "I've helped out Chloe before at lambing season, and I thought you'd enjoy it. What do you think?"

"It's a lot of work, but it's fun, too," Chloe told Charles. "He'll need a bottle every couple of hours, and you'll need to keep him warm and quiet."

"But why can't his mom take care of him?" Charles asked.

Chloe bit her lip. "Well, she had three lambs," she said. "And she can really only feed and take care of two. So this one was kind of—left out, I guess." She shook her head sadly as she looked down at the lamb in her arms. "It happens every year. If we bottle-feed them and take good care of them, they can usually rejoin the flock after a while."

Charles looked at Steve. "What about Freckles?"

Steve shrugged. "I think we can work it out." He explained to Chloe about the puppy. "It's that one who's been floating around as a stray," he said. "We're just taking care of him for a few days until he gets back on his feet. Then we'll find him a home. He's a good pup, not a mean bone in his body. I think if we keep them separate it'll be okay."

Chloe nodded. She seemed distracted. "Look, I've got to get back in the barn. I'm expecting more lambs any minute. I packed up a bunch of supplies for you." She jutted her chin at a cloth grocery bag near the gate.

Steve grabbed the bag. "Charles, why don't you take the lamb?" he said.

Charles's eyes grew wide. "Me?" he asked.

CHAPTER SIX

Charles looked up at Dad, and Dad grinned and shrugged.

"Yes, you," said Chloe. "Come on in here and I'll hand him off. You can zip him up inside your jacket to keep him warm."

Charles walked up to the gate, but he couldn't quite make himself open it and go inside. Some of the sheep in the pen were really big, with huge curled horns.

"They're all gentle," said Chloe, as if she had read his mind. "No worries. I promise they won't hurt you."

Dad helped Charles unlatch the gate, and he

walked inside, stepping nervously around the sheep that milled about. Now he could see that there were lambs in the pen, too. They had been sticking close to their mothers, but when they saw him they ran and jumped and dodged here and there, as if they were calling out "Chase me, chase me!" Charles was dying to hold one of them, but they didn't look like they'd be at all easy to catch. In the middle of the flock stood Chloe, holding the littlest lamb of all. Charles walked closer. The lamb's tiny ears twitched and his mouth worked. He made a soft bleating noise that went straight to Charles's heart.

"Ready?" said Chloe when Charles was right in front of her. Charles held out his arms, and she nestled the soft, warm lamb into them. "There you go," she said.

Charles gulped and held the lamb tight. Was Chloe actually handing him this helpless, hungry, frightened baby animal? Charles didn't know anything about taking care of lambs. What was he supposed to do? He tightened his grip, took a few quick, shallow breaths, and looked over at his dad. Dad grinned at him and gave him a thumbs-up. Charles hugged the lamb close, and felt tears come to his eyes.

"Don't worry, little guy," he whispered to the lamb. "We'll take good care of you."

When Charles climbed into Steve's truck, with the lamb zipped inside his jacket, Freckles sat up straight. His ears perked up, the brown one a little higher than the freckled one, and his nose wiggled as he sniffed the air.

What's this? What's this I smell?

Then the pup leaned over and began to sniff Charles. The lamb, nestled deep inside his jacket, began to bleat. Charles could feel him trembling—just the way Freckles had trembled when they had first found him.

"Dad!" Charles said. "Can you take Freckles up front? I think he's scaring Fluffy."

"Fluffy?" Dad turned around in his seat, raising his eyebrows. "You're quick with the names, aren't you?" He smiled as he reached back to pick up Freckles. "Come on, dude. Ride up here with me," he said as he held the curious puppy firmly. Freckles looked back at the lamb and whined softly.

I just want to be friends. What's the big deal?

"Well, this lamb actually is very fluffy," said Charles. He couldn't get over how soft the lamb's coat had felt in his hands. It was like petting a cloud.

"I'm sure he is," said Steve. "All lambs are. I think it's the perfect name for a baby lamb— especially this baby lamb."

Fluffy never really stopped bleating all the way back to Steve's, and he bleated the whole time as they hiked through the woods to the cabin. The sound hurt Charles's ears. It made Charles's heart hurt, too, to hear the sad, lonely way the lamb was crying. Fluffy's mood seemed to match the low, gray skies overhead. "Poor guy! He must miss his mom," he said to Dad. "And his brother and sister."

"I think he's mainly hungry," said Steve as they came into the cabin. "I'm sure you can make him feel at home while I get a bottle ready. Sit down on the couch with him, and get comfortable."

Steve was rummaging through the bag Chloe had packed. He pulled out a bag of disposable diapers. "Better put one of these on him," he said, handing it to Dad. He laughed when he saw the look on Charles's face.

"It's what we do when we take care of baby lambs inside a house," Steve said. "Baby lambs, well"—he lowered his voice to a whisper—"they go to the bathroom an awful lot!"

He returned to rummaging in the bag. "Chloe probably packed some special lamb milk replacement formula and a bottle. It's easy to mix this stuff up, and the lambs love it." He pulled out the bottle. "Ta-da!" Then he reached back in for a plastic zipper bag full of yellowish powder. "And here's the formula. Great."

Charles could feel the lamb's heart beating super fast inside his chest. He was still bleating, but the sound was growing weaker. The lamb's ears hung down limply, and he did not try to struggle out of Charles's arms. He just lay there, still trembling. "I think he wore himself out with all that crying," Charles said. He gazed down at the soft, tiny animal and felt hot tears come to his eyes. The poor thing!

"He'll be fine once we get him fed," said Steve, who had been bustling around in the kitchen. He came over to the couch with the bottle he'd prepared. "I hope he's already learned how to drink from the bottle. Let's see how he does."

The lamb stopped bleating as soon as he saw the bottle. Right away, he stretched out his neck and began sucking hard. His little tail wagged as he tugged at the nipple. Charles had to hold tight to keep the lamb from pulling the bottle right out of his hands. "Wow!" said Charles. "You were right. He sure is hungry."

That reminded him. "I bet Freckles is hungry, too," he said. "Did he have breakfast? Hey, where *is* Freckles?" Charles had been so focused on the

lamb that—for a few moments—he'd almost forgotten all about the adorable little mutt.

"He's just outside the door," Dad said. "I left him
in the mudroom until we could get the lamb settled in. He seems awfully interested in Fluffy."

"I think you can bring him in now," said Steve.
"Just hang on to him and let him sniff around a
bit. Freckles needs to get used to the idea that we
have another guest staying with us, and Fluffy
needs to get used to the idea of dogs. Let's just do
our best to keep them apart, though."

Charles wasn't sure how easy that was going to
be in the tiny cabin. But he knew Steve was right.
It was better to give both of these young animals
lots of quiet time. They had been through so much
already.

Dad went outside and came right back in, with
Freckles on a leash. The spotted pup was on alert;
he obviously knew there was another creature in

the cabin. His ears were perked up, and he wagged his tail as he sniffed all around.

Where is he? What is he? Is he friendly? I could really use a pal.

Freckles dragged Dad straight to the couch where Charles and Steve were sitting with the lamb. Charles hugged the lamb closer in case he was afraid, but Fluffy was concentrating so hard on eating that he didn't even seem to notice the nosy puppy. He wasn't trembling anymore, Charles noticed. He had relaxed into Charles's arms as he sucked on the bottle.

"Freckles!" Dad said, pulling on the leash. "Leave the lamb alone. He needs to settle in without your help." He took Freckles over to the kitchen and poured some kibble into his bowl. "I don't know, Steve. Looks like we really have our hands full here. And there's still the sugaring to do."

Steve cleared his throat. "Yup, and there's one other thing," he said, gesturing to the window. "I forgot to mention the news I heard at the post office, about a big fast-moving snowstorm coming our way. The weather people are predicting a foot or more during the day today, and overnight."

"What?" Dad asked.

Steve nodded at the window. "Looks to me like it's already started."

Charles looked out the window. "Wow!" he said. Steve was right. Giant flakes were spinning through the air, carried by gusting winds that tossed the branches on the trees. He felt like the cabin was inside a snow globe that some giant had just shaken. Steve didn't seem to think it was a big deal, but Charles knew that back at home, a snowstorm like this would close the schools and roads.

"That's March in Vermont for you," Steve said. "You never know what's around the corner. The weather can change in minutes. On the plus side," he added, "if it's cold enough to snow, the sap probably won't be running today, so we don't have to go around and empty buckets. We can finish boiling off what we already have in the tank and then just batten down the hatches and get cozy for the night."

"You mean—" Dad began.

Steve nodded. "I think it's best if you two stay here with me tonight. Between the snow and the critters, I think I could probably use some help."

Charles smiled and hugged the sleeping lamb on his lap. This was turning out to be the best spring vacation ever.

CHAPTER SEVEN

Charles spent the whole rest of the afternoon in the cabin. The wind howled and the snow swirled outside, but inside it was warm and cozy. Charles was happy to take care of Fluffy while Dad and Steve finished boiling up the sap in the tank. Freckles mostly stayed outside with them, though he barked at the door now and then to see if Fluffy was ready to play.

It turned out that Steve had been right about Fluffy being fine once he'd had some formula. The lamb stopped trembling and bleating, and by the time he finished the first bottle he was ready to get down off Charles's lap and explore the cabin. He was so cute as he scampered around on his tiny hooves. He checked everything out, from the plants on the windowsill to the stack of CDs by the bookcase. His tail wagged just like a dog's as he pawed at things that interested him, and his little ears moved around like radar antennae. And boy, could he jump. The first time Charles saw Fluffy leap onto the couch, he was shocked. It was like the lamb had little springs in his feet, and he loved to bounce around. Once, when Charles was down on all fours trying to play with him, Fluffy even bounced right onto Charles's back!

When the lamb began bleating again, Charles knew exactly what to do. "Food is coming," he told Fluffy. "Hold on just a sec." Steve had showed him how to mix the formula. Charles quickly made up a bottle, then took it over to the couch and held it while Fluffy sucked hungrily on the nipple. Charles loved holding Fluffy while he ate. The lamb's curly coat was so springy and soft, and it was so entertaining to watch his little nose wriggle and his little ears swivel this way and that.

This time when he finished eating, Fluffy curled up on Charles's lap and went right to sleep. "Nap time for little lambies," Charles whispered, as he stroked the lamb's soft coat. "That's right. You need your rest." Fluffy sighed and nestled in more comfortably. Charles kissed the top of his head. Fluffy smelled so good—kind of woolly, actually, like Charles's favorite red sweater.

A few minutes later, Charles's stomach began to growl. He'd been so busy feeding Fluffy that he'd forgotten to feed himself. But now he was stuck sitting there on the couch until the lamb woke up. Charles tried to ignore his grumbling tummy, but all he could think about was the giant sandwich he was going to make as soon as he could.

Finally, Fluffy woke up. He blinked at Charles,

then gave himself a little shake and leapt down onto the floor to continue his explorations. Charles jumped up, too, and headed straight for the kitchen. If he was hungry, Dad and Steve must be, too. He made three big sandwiches and gobbled down half of his own while he mixed another bottle of formula. He knew that Fluffy was probably going to start bleating any minute, so he might as well be ready.

Sure enough, Charles had barely finished getting the formula mixed before Fluffy began to bleat again. Sighing, Charles grabbed one more bite of sandwich, then brought the bottle over to the couch. The lamb jumped right up and began to drink as if he was starving. This time, when Fluffy finished the bottle, Charles settled the lamb between some pillows on the couch. He loved having Fluffy sleep on his lap, but he didn't want to get trapped again. "I've got to bring lunch out to Dad and Steve," he said to Fluffy. "You be a good lambie and have a nice nap. I'll be right back."

Charles put the sandwiches on a plate and pulled on his boots. When he pushed the back door open, he gasped. Swirling snow surrounded him, the wind pushing flakes into his eyes, his nose, his mouth. "Wow!" he said. He could hardly even make out the sugar shack through the curtain of white.

Then he saw something moving, brown spots against the white. "Freckles!" he said. The puppy bounded happily through the snow toward him, ears flapping. He didn't seem at all fazed by the blizzard.

Freckles sniffed at the plate in Charles's hands. He gave Charles a sideways look and a grin, wagging his tail hopefully.

Maybe you've got some treats for me there?

76

Charles smiled and shook his head at the little brown-and-white pup. Freckles already seemed completely at home here. It was too bad that Steve didn't want any pets. "This is for the people, Freckles," he said. "But if you want to come inside with me after I deliver it, I'll give you some kibble." Charles knew Freckles wouldn't understand everything he was saying, but it didn't matter. Dogs liked it when you talked to them and explained things.

Charles pushed on, stomping through the snow toward the sugar shack. The sap was boiling hard, and Charles could smell the sweet scent of almost-syrup.

"Hurray!" said Steve when he saw Charles coming. He was chopping wood, but he put down his hatchet and came over to take a sandwich. He brushed the snow off his jacket and smiled at Charles. "Our hero. I'm starving."

"So am I," Dad said. He stoked the fire one more time, throwing chunks of wood into the roaring blaze beneath the boiling sap. Then he stood up and helped himself, taking half a sandwich in each hand. "Thanks a lot, Charles." He took a big bite of the one in his right hand. "Yum! You're getting good at this. Maybe I'll start asking you to make my lunches when we're home."

Charles ducked his head. He liked making Dad happy.

"We've already made three gallons of syrup," Steve reported. "Just a bit more to boil off and we'll be done for the day."

"How's the lamb doing?" Dad asked. "I mean, Fluffy."

"He's great. He's already had three bottles," said Charles.

"Nice work," said Steve. "I knew you'd be good at this."

Charles ducked his head again. "He's probably hungry again by now," he said. "I better get back in there." He was beginning to realize what a big responsibility it was to take care of a baby lamb. No wonder Steve had been happy for the help. Charles hurried through the snow and let himself back into the cabin. It was a relief to shut the door and leave the snow and wind outside.

It was quiet inside the cabin, very quiet. Charles did not hear any bleating. That was good. Maybe Fluffy was still napping. But where was he? The lamb was not on the couch where Charles had last seen him.

"Where are you?" he called, looking all around for Fluffy. Then he spotted the little lamb, curled up on the bed of towels near the woodstove—with Freckles right next to him.

"Oh, no!" Charles said. Steve had told him to keep the animals apart. How could this have happened? Had the wind pushed the door open? Maybe Charles hadn't latched it all the way when he went out. He rushed over, ready to pull Freckles away. But as he got closer, he saw that there was no need to worry. The lamb and the puppy both looked perfectly happy curled up together. It was obvious that Freckles wasn't going to hurt Fluffy. The lamb's eyes were almost closed, and he had that funny smiling expression on his face. Freckles was relaxed, lying with one paw over his new friend's shoulder. The pup looked up at Charles and thumped his tail.

I found myself a buddy. Isn't he the best?

Charles smiled at Freckles and bent to pet him. "Good boy," he said. "That's a good, gentle boy." At that, Fluffy leapt to his feet and began bleating. Charles burst out laughing. "Yes, Fluffy. You're a good boy, too. But you're a lamb, not a puppy, remember?"

Fluffy bleated and pranced, sproinging around the room. Freckles scrambled after him, and the two animals had a quick game of chase. First Fluffy chased Freckles, then Freckles chased Fluffy until Fluffy won the game by jumping up onto the back of the couch, and from there to the top of a low bookshelf. Freckles stared up at his new friend, panting. Then he went into a play bow, front paws outstretched and hind end in the air.

C'mon down from there and chase me some more!

But Fluffy suddenly seemed to remember that he was hungry. He began to bleat again and didn't stop until Charles fixed him a bottle and brought it over to the couch. Fluffy leapt from the bookshelf down onto the couch, and then onto Charles's lap. He began to drink hungrily, while Freckles lay down to watch.

Soon after the bottle was empty, Fluffy fell fast asleep on Charles's lap. Freckles snoozed, too, at Charles's feet. "Whew," whispered Charles to himself, leaning back on the couch. It was a lot of work taking care of these animals! He was ready for a rest himself.

CHAPTER EIGHT

Charles didn't mean to fall asleep. But the next thing he knew, Freckles was chasing Fluffy around the cabin again.

"What is going *on* in here?" said Dad, who must have just come in. He stood by the front door, pulling off his jacket and boots. "Freckles, stop that! You're scaring the lamb."

Charles laughed. "Fluffy isn't scared of anything," he said. "They're playing. Just watch for another minute and you'll see." Sure enough, a moment later the two reversed directions and Fluffy began chasing Freckles. The puppy scrambled here and there, sliding on the wooden floor, while the lamb bounced after him.

Dad started to laugh. "Just like a pair of puppies," he said. "I guess lambs are playful, too."

"Oh, sure," said Steve, who had come in behind Dad, stomping snow off his boots. "I love to watch them over at Chloe's when they're first let out to pasture. The lambs are all over the place, climbing on everything—including their mothers! They chase each other just like that."

"I thought we were supposed to keep them apart," said Charles. He'd been feeling terrible about maybe leaving the door open so Freckles could slip inside.

"Well, we did our best, and then I guess they took over. If they want to be friends, who are we to stop them?" Steve said. Nothing ever seemed to upset him. "Now, are you ready to help me get supper?"

Charles jumped up. "Sure," he said. His only

regular chores at home were setting the table and clearing the table. He and Lizzie traded days on that. He didn't usually help to make dinner, but why not? If Steve thought he could, Charles was ready to give it a try. At home, Charles was just a kid. Here at Steve's, he felt like one of the guys.

"Wash your hands," said Steve. "Then maybe the first thing you should do is get another bottle of formula mixed up. Seems like this lamb gets hungry every couple hours or so. We might as well be ready."

Steve was right; no sooner had Charles finished getting the bottle ready than Fluffy started to bleat. "I'll feed him this time," said Dad. He sat down on the couch and Fluffy leapt right onto his lap. "Whoa!" Dad looked surprised. Then he gave Fluffy a hug. "This guy learned fast, didn't he?" Charles gave Dad the bottle, and Fluffy began to drink.

"That's right, fella," said Dad. "Drink up." Charles watched, smiling. Dad had the same happy, dreamy look on his face that he got when he was holding a human baby. Dad loved babies.

Charles went back into the kitchen, and Steve put him to work peeling potatoes. "The peeler's sharp," he said. "So watch your fingers."

At home, Mom didn't usually let Charles use sharp knives or peelers on his own. Charles picked up the peeler and swiped it along the potato the way Steve had shown him, being careful to keep his fingertips out of the way. It wasn't hard at all.

"Now we slice them, real nice and thin," said Steve. He demonstrated for Charles, then handed him a long knife. Charles glanced at Dad, but Dad was still staring down at Fluffy with that goofy look on his face. He shrugged and began to slice. Before long, he'd sliced up eight potatoes.

"Nicely done," said Steve, who was busy mixing up meat loaf. "Now we lay them in this baking dish, one partly on top of the next, so they look kind of like fish scales."

Charles was getting the hang of this cooking thing. It was easy—and a lot of fun. He laid out the potatoes, then added salt, pepper, butter, and milk the way Steve told him to. Then they popped the pan into the oven that Steve had preheated. "That's it," said Steve, giving Charles a high five. "You just made scalloped potatoes the way my grandma taught me to when I was your age."

Charles grinned. He looked over at Dad and saw that his father was snoring, with his head drooping over the sleeping lamb nestled on his lap. Freckles lay at Dad's feet, also snoozing. Charles put his hand over his mouth to quiet his laughter, then tugged on Steve's sleeve and pointed.

The best part about helping to make dinner

was sitting down to eat it. It was just about the most delicious dinner Charles had ever had, and Dad couldn't stop talking about how great the scalloped potatoes were. Charles didn't even mind helping to clean up afterward. Everything seemed like fun here at Steve's cabin. He was secretly glad that the snowstorm had come. This was so much cozier than another night at the inn.

After they'd cleaned up, Steve suggested they take Freckles out for a walk before bedtime. "Wouldn't want the pup to wander off in this storm," he said as he snapped on a leash.

Fluffy woke up and wanted to come along, but Dad held on to the lamb as Steve and Charles stepped outside. "Wow!" said Charles when he saw how deep the snow already was. It came up over his boots as soon as he stepped out of the mudroom.

"I know," said Steve. "And it's still coming down

hard. I think we might be caring for Fluffy for longer than we thought. I doubt anybody's going anywhere tomorrow."

Freckles plunged into the snow. Even with the flashlight beam on him, he almost disappeared into the whiteness, except for his brown freckles and his one brown ear. He bounded and leapt, pushing his way through the drifts, as Steve and Charles tried to follow the old snowshoe trail.

"Good enough," said Steve after Freckles had done his business. "Let's head back."

The cabin felt warmer and cozier than ever when they came back in, brushing snow off their jackets. The yellow glow of the kerosene lamps made everything look pretty. "Fluffy missed you," Dad said. The lamb leapt off his lap when he spotted Freckles, and the two began to play again. This time, they both seemed tired out after a few laps around the room. Charles gave Fluffy one more bottle before bedtime and helped Dad change his diaper. Then he got the bed of towels near the woodstove all ready for Fluffy and Freckles. Charles was sleeping on the floor right next to them, on an old camping mat of Steve's. Dad was going to sleep on the couch.

Charles sat down on the floor by the woodstove to give Fluffy one more hug before he tucked the lamb in. The lamb was so soft and warm, and he smelled so good. He nuzzled Charles's cheek and bleated softly into his ear. "I love you too, Fluffy," Charles said, holding him close. Then he felt something nudging his elbow. It was Freckles, pushing his nose against Charles's arm.

What about me? Don't I get a hug?

Charles smiled. He had been as patient as he could be, and now Freckles was finally ready for a hug. He settled Fluffy onto his bed of towels, then pulled Freckles gently onto his lap. The white pup was warm and relaxed, and he let Charles hold him close without squirming or pulling away. Charles felt tears welling up in his eyes as he kissed the top of the puppy's sweet-smelling head. Lambs were wonderful, but there was nothing like hugging a puppy.

"We can all take turns feeding Fluffy when he wakes up hungry in the night," said Steve as he turned off the lamps and climbed up the ladder to his sleeping loft. "I'll make up a few bottles so they're ready."

Charles slid down into the warm sleeping bag a little later on, feeling happy to lie down and stretch out. It had been a long, exciting day. He couldn't wait to see how much more snow fell overnight. Maybe Steve had a sled he could borrow to use on that hill beyond the last row of maples. Drowsily, Charles glanced over at Freckles and Fluffy, who lay curled up together nearby. They looked so cozy in the flickering light from the woodstove's glass window. Charles yawned and slipped off into a deep sleep.

It seemed like only minutes before Fluffy began to bleat again. Charles rolled over in his sleeping bag, groaning. How could one tiny lamb eat so much?

"I've got it," Steve said. Charles heard him climbing down the ladder from his sleeping loft. Soon, Fluffy's bleating stopped as he gulped down the bottle Steve fed him. Charles watched them for a while by the light of the woodstove, then drifted off to sleep again.

When he woke, there was a milky-white light coming from the windows. Charles rubbed his eyes. He had slept through the whole night! Dad was still snoring on the couch, and Steve was up in his loft. Why hadn't any of them heard Fluffy bleating for food again? Charles sat up straight and looked over at the little bed near the stove.

It was empty.

"Dad!" he called, jumping to his feet. "Steve! Wake up! Fluffy and Freckles are missing."

CHAPTER NINE

Steve scrambled down the ladder. Dad leapt off the couch. "What? Where?" Dad said, rubbing his eyes. "How?"

Steve was already pulling his boots and jacket on. "I woke up in the middle of the night and went out to check on the snow. Maybe they slipped out behind me?"

Charles slid out of the sleeping bag and ran for his own jacket and boots. A moment later, he and Dad and Steve were all outside, yelling for Freckles and Fluffy.

The snow was still coming down, swirling out of the dim early-morning sky. Charles followed

94

Steve from the back door to the sugaring shed. The heavy, wet snow came up above his knees. It was tough going, slogging through the drifts.

"Where'd they go?" Steve asked, waving his arms. His face was red and his eyes were wide.

"We'll find them," Charles said. "We have to find them." He had never seen Steve look upset before. He pictured the little puppy and the soft, baby lamb floundering through the snow and his heart sank. This was exactly the kind of thing Dad had meant about why Steve didn't want pets. Too much responsibility.

"They're not around back," Dad said, coming from the other side of the cabin. "I didn't see any tracks at all."

"Okay," said Steve. He took a few deep breaths, as if to calm himself. "We'll have to search farther from the house. We'll need snowshoes." He headed for the cabin, then stopped short when he came close to the door. "Oh, no," he said, stooping over to look more closely. "The poor little guy."

"What is it?" Charles asked. He and his dad joined Steve by the door.

"Someone tried to get our attention," Steve said, pointing to the bottom of the door. At one corner the blue paint was scratched all the way down to bare wood.

Charles felt his heart skip a beat. "That must have been Freckles, scratching to be let in," he said.

"Exactly," said Steve. "They got out, but then they couldn't get back inside."

"And I bet Fluffy was bleating, too," said Dad. "How could we have slept through that?"

Steve grunted and stood up. "We were really tired," he said. "And the sound of the wind must have been louder. Anyway, we didn't hear them. Now we have to find them." He grabbed snowshoes from their hooks inside the mudroom and handed them around.

"But how do we know where to look? There aren't any tracks to follow," Dad said. "The storm wiped them out."

"And *we* wiped them out," said Charles, suddenly realizing what had happened. "We can't see any tracks right around here because we ran around and messed everything up. Maybe if we just go a little bit farther we'll see something."

"Just what I was thinking," said Steve as he buckled on his snowshoes. "Let's go." He plunged off into the snow. A moment later, Dad and Charles followed.

It was not easy, slogging through the deep snow. Charles's snowshoes punched through the heavy, wet drifts no matter how carefully he tried to walk. He felt like he was tripping over his own feet. He had to lift his knees high for each step, as if he was marching. The snow melted around the tops of his boots, and his wet socks squelched as he walked. It was exhausting.

"Take it easy, sport," said Dad from behind him. Dad was breathing hard, too. "Don't try to rush; that only makes it harder."

But Charles felt like he had to rush. If he felt cold and wet and tired and frustrated, think how those two baby animals must feel, out there on their own!

"I think I see tracks," Steve shouted. Charles saw him stoop over, then kneel down in the snow. "Yes!"

Charles and Dad caught up to him, and Steve showed them the indentations in the snow. "They're blurry because the snow is still falling. But I'm almost sure these are recent."

"I don't get it," Dad said. "Why would they

wander even farther away from the house? I mean, here they are, out in a howling snowstorm. Wouldn't you think they would try to find shelter?"

Charles stared at Dad. "That's it!" he said.

Steve looked confused for a moment, then his face lit up and he nodded at Charles. "You're right!" He stood up. "Let's go."

Dad didn't get it yet. "Go where?" he asked.

To Charles it was so obvious. If the animals needed shelter, Freckles knew where to find it. That's where he would have gone. That's where he would have taken his friend. "To the cave, to the place where we first found Freckles," Charles said, following Steve up the trail.

Sure enough, the blurry tracks turned off the main trail toward the pine forest, just as they had on that first day. Steve was charging through the snow now, and Charles and Dad struggled to keep up.

The snow wasn't as deep once they were in the woods, where the long boughs of the pine trees had caught the falling flakes. As Steve pushed through, drifts of snow fell from the branches, slipping down Charles's neck and making him shiver. He didn't care. They were getting closer.

"Freckles!" he called. "We're coming!"

When they entered the small clearing near the rocky ledge, Charles tried to dash ahead. He couldn't wait to see Freckles's face sticking out from the little cave opening.

"Wait," said Steve, grabbing Charles's jacket. "Don't scare them."

Charles slowed down. He knew Steve was right. Even though Freckles and Fluffy had gotten used to people—and even liked being around them— they were probably very frightened right now.

Dad came up behind them, and Charles put a finger to his lips. Dad nodded. All three of them crept quietly forward until they were close to the rocky ledge. Charles held his breath. There! There, in the dark little cave opening, Charles saw a flash of white, a spot of brown.

Steve motioned for them to stop. He knelt down, and so did Charles and Dad. "Hey, friends," Steve said softly. "It's us. We're here to help."

Charles saw Freckles poke his whole head out of the cave. And, just behind him, he saw Fluffy's adorable face, with its sticking-out ears! "It's okay," he whispered. "Don't be scared."

That was when Fluffy pushed right past Freckles and bounded into the clearing, bleating happily. Or maybe hungrily. Or probably both.

Charles picked the lamb up and held him close. "There you are," he said. "You're safe with us."

Now Freckles ran out, too—straight for Steve.

I thought you'd never find us!

Steve laughed as he scooped the little dog into his arms and hugged him. "You rascal," he said. "Running off like that. You had us worried."

"But he was smart to come here," said Charles. "He knew just what to do to take care of himself and his friend."

"Let's get both of these friends home," said Dad. "I bet they're hungry and cold and tired." He helped Charles zip Fluffy inside his jacket, where the lamb would be cozy, and then all three of them trudged back to the cabin, carrying their precious cargo.

When they got inside, Charles rubbed Fluffy down with one of the towels while Steve dried Freckles. Dad brought over a bottle, and Charles sat right down by the woodstove to feed the bleating lamb. "That's right," he said as Fluffy sucked at the bottle. "You're safe now." Freckles curled up next to them, gazing lovingly at his woolly friend.

Steve got up to pour out some kibble for Freckles. "Come on, pup," he called. "You must be hungry, too."

Freckles glanced over at his dish and thumped his tail, but he didn't budge.

I'm good for now. Just want to make sure my friend is okay.

Charles felt the lamb relax in his arms. The bottle was nearly empty, and Fluffy's eyelids were drooping. Soon it would be nap time again. Charles sighed and let himself relax, too. He was so glad that both animals were safe and sound in the cabin.

"Look," said Steve. He pointed out the window,

and Charles saw a patch of blue. "The snow has finally stopped. The wind has died down, too. I think the sun might even come out." He grinned at Dad and Charles. "You know what that means? The trees will start running again. More sap to gather."

CHAPTER TEN

The rest of that day passed much like the day before: Steve and Dad gathered sap and boiled it while Charles looked after the animals. He made sandwiches again at lunchtime and brought them out to the sugar shed. By late afternoon, it was obvious that Charles and Dad would be spending one more night at the cabin; Steve really needed their help.

The next morning, Charles was giving Fluffy a bottle when he heard a groan from the kitchen. "Oh, no!" said Steve. He smacked his head. "I don't believe it."

"What happened?" Charles asked.

"I just checked the calendar, that's what," said Steve. "We've been so busy, I spaced it out. But this is Maple Open House Weekend. That means today's the day of the Spring Fling Wing-Ding!"

Charles remembered that the Spring Fling was the annual party dad had told him about on the way up. "What's Maple Open House Weekend?" he asked.

"Sugarhouses all over the state invite visitors to stop by one weekend in March," Steve said. "I just like to add to the fun by having a big party for my friends, as well."

"Will people still come, even with all this snow?" Dad asked Steve.

Steve laughed. "By this time of year, Vermonters have what we call cabin fever from being stuck inside all winter. Everybody's happy to get out and do something different. They'll be here." He pulled the fridge open. "I'm going to have to go shopping," he said, looking inside. "There's barely enough food left for us, much less twenty other people."

"Doesn't everybody bring food to the party?" Dad asked.

Steve nodded. "Sure. But I like to have plenty on hand, too. I was hoping you'd make your famous firehouse chili—I already bought the ingredients for that."

"Perfect," said Dad. "Now that Charles is becoming a great chef, he can help me cook while you're shopping. We can tidy up the place, too."

"Really?" Steve asked, looking relieved. "That would be excellent. As far as gathering sap and boiling, we can do that when everyone's here. People love to help out. It's part of the fun."

The rest of the morning went by in a blur. Charles helped Dad chop onions, open cans of beans, and add spices. He put away the sleeping bag and the blankets Dad had been using, and shook out the towels that Fluffy and Freckles had been sleeping on. In between, he gave Fluffy a bottle every time he began to bleat, took Freckles outside when he asked to be let out, changed the lamb's diaper, and tried to keep Fluffy from jumping onto the furniture he'd just dusted.

By the time Steve came back, the cabin was tidy and a big pot of chili was bubbling away. "Mmmm, it smells fantastic in here," said Steve as he set bags of groceries on the counter. "And it looks terrific, too. I can't thank you two enough."

People started arriving at lunchtime, and Charles stayed busy passing out bowls of chili and helping to set out the rest of the food the guests had bought. Fluffy and Freckles greeted each guest happily, bouncing around like pinballs in a machine. As the afternoon went on and it began to warm up outside, the party moved to the sugar shack, where Steve had started to boil sap.

The food was spread out on a picnic table, and people of all ages stood around to watch the sap boil while they caught up after the long winter. A couple of other dogs had arrived, too, and Charles was happy to see that Freckles gave each of them a friendly greeting.

Chloe arrived and Charles took her inside to see Fluffy. "Wow, you've been doing a great job with this one," she said. "He is really thriving."

Charles smiled. "He's a good eater," he told her. "We're already almost out of formula."

"No problem," said Chloe. "My last ewe had her lamb yesterday and all the babies are doing well. I'll be able to bring him home with me today, now that I can take care of him. He needs to be back with the flock, anyway. It's time he remembered that he's actually a sheep, not a puppy."

Charles gulped. He'd known all along that Fluffy would be going back to the farm, but still.

He was going to miss the little lamb, and Freckles was going to miss his friend even more. But Chloe was right. Fluffy belonged with the other sheep.

"Speaking of puppies," said Charles as he ladled out a bowl of chili for Chloe. "We're looking for a home for Freckles. He's really smart, and great with lambs. Maybe you could use him on the farm?" Charles had decided that Chloe's farm would be a perfect home for Freckles, and he'd been planning this speech all morning. "That way, he and Fluffy would always be together," he finished.

Chloe ruffled Freckles's ears. "Oh, I really wish I could. He's a real cutie, and he'd be welcome to visit with us anytime. But I already have Sky and Galena, my two sheepdogs. Between them and the sheep and the goats and the geese and ducks and chickens and my milk cow, I think my farm is just about full up."

"I didn't know you had all those animals," said Charles. "I only saw the sheep the day we came to get Fluffy."

"Come visit before you leave," Chloe said. "You can meet them all. Meanwhile, maybe Adelaide would be interested in the pup. After all, she fed him all winter while he lived in her barn." She and Charles walked outside, and Chloe pointed out a pretty white-haired woman with glasses.

Charles took a plate of cheese and crackers and started to walk around, offering it to people. When he got to Adelaide, he smiled up at her. "What do you think of Freckles?" he asked. "I know he was staying in your barn for a while. He looks good, doesn't he?"

"Is that what you named the pup?" she asked,

taking a cracker. "Great name. I love it. And yes, he looks great. Steve told me you've been taking really good care of him. I couldn't even get close to him when he was staying in my barn. He was too shy."

"He's not so shy anymore," said Charles. "Freckles even likes hugs and belly rubs now."

"Sweet," said Adelaide. "I'd love to pet him, but I'm so allergic that I'd be sneezing for the rest of the day."

Charles sighed. He had just been about to ask Adelaide if she wanted to adopt Freckles, but now there was no point. "Freckles really needs a home," said Charles.

"What about Steve?" asked Adelaide.

"Steve?" Charles was surprised. "I thought he didn't want any pets."

Adelaide laughed. "Oh, no, you're absolutely right about that. I can't imagine Steve with a dog. A very independent cat, maybe—but never a dog. No, I meant the other Steve. Dancing Steve. That one." She pointed to a man with a big bushy beard and mustache.

"Dancing Steve?" Charles asked.

Adelaide laughed again. "That's what we call him. He loves to go dancing and he does it whenever he can."

"Okay." Charles shrugged. "So maybe Dancing Steve wants a dog." He went to pick up a platter of deviled eggs to carry through the crowd, weaving this way and that, until he was standing next to the man with the beard.

"You must be Paul's son," said Dancing Steve, sticking out his hand for a shake. "I hear you did a great job taking care of Chloe's lamb."

"Um, thanks," said Charles. "Egg?" He held up the platter, and Dancing Steve helped himself. Charles decided to get right to the point. "Did you know that Freckles needs a home?" he asked, pointing to the happy pup. At the moment, Freckles was playing with a dog who had a thick brown-and-black coat. "Adelaide said you might be interested."

Dancing Steve watched the dogs play. "Well, if I wanted to have two dogs, I might be," he said. "He seems to get along well with June." He nodded at the brown-and-black dog. "That's my dog, June. But I've got a busy life, so I'm a one-dog man." He smiled apologetically. "Sorry," he said. "Keep trying! There are lots of dog lovers here." He pointed Charles to a couple named Eric and Patty.

Eric and Patty pointed to Karl and Tracy. Tracy pointed to Jake. Jake pointed to Danny and Mary. Danny pointed to David. David pointed to Elsa.

Nobody wanted a dog.

By the time the party wound down and the last guests headed up the trail, Charles was tired and discouraged.

"You okay?" Steve asked as they carried dirty

dishes into the cabin. "I know you'll miss Fluffy." Chloe had taken the lamb home with her, and Charles already did miss him. He missed watching him jump around, he missed giving him bottles—he even missed changing his diaper! He could tell that Freckles missed his friend, too. The white pup lay on the bed near the woodstove, his chin on his paws.

Charles shrugged. "I do miss Fluffy, but it's not just that. I asked pretty much every one of the guests today whether they'd like to adopt Freckles, and I still haven't found him a forever home," he said.

Steve put down a pile of dishes and wiped his hands on a dish towel. "You didn't ask me," he said.

Charles stared at him. "Because you don't want a dog," he said. "I mean, that's what everybody says, anyway."

"Well, it's true. I don't want just any dog," said

Steve. "But sometimes the right dog just happens to come along. A smart dog. A loving dog. A helpful dog. A brave and independent dog . . . a *good* dog."

When Freckles heard the words "good dog," he jumped up and trotted over to Steve. He leaned against Steve's leg and gazed up at him, wagging his tail.

That's me! I'm a good dog.

Steve gazed back at Freckles and scratched the top of the puppy's head. "That's right," he said. "You really are a good dog. So, how would you like to be my dog?"

Charles held his breath for a second. Then he let it all out in a burst. "Really?" he asked. "That would be—that would be—"

"It would be fantastic!" said Dad. "Are you sure you're ready for the responsibility?"

Steve smiled. "This guy is no trouble at all. He and I are going to be best pals. It's about time this hermit had some company." He ruffled Freckles's ears. "What do you say, friend?"

Freckles licked Steve's hand and thumped his tail.

I'm happy to be home at last.

"And he can go visit Fluffy whenever he wants!" Charles said. He couldn't stop smiling as he helped Steve and Dad clean up, and he was still smiling as he and Dad headed off down the path for the very last time later that day, their backpacks heavy with jars of sweet, golden-brown maple syrup. It was hard to say good-bye to Steve and Freckles, but Charles knew that the spotted pup could not have found a more perfect home.

PUPPY TIPS

It might surprise you to know that some puppies are shy, like Freckles. Not all puppies are ready to climb into your lap, be hugged, or even be petted. This might be because they've already had a tough life, like Freckles, or because they are naturally shy. The important thing is to give a shy puppy time to get to know you. Be patient, the way Charles was with Freckles. Don't frighten the puppy by trying to hug him too soon. Let him sniff you, and make sure that every interaction is positive and calm. No yelling, no bouncing around, no grabbing, no sudden movements. Not all dogs like to be hugged, but given time, most puppies and dogs will come to enjoy being petted and loved.

Dear Reader,

I enjoyed writing this book because sugaring time is one of my favorite times of year. I spend many days out in the snowy Vermont woods every March and April, helping my friend Steve and his family and friends to make maple syrup. It's hard work but, as Charles discovered, it's also a lot of fun. My dog, Zipper, loves to come along and play with other helpers' dogs, especially his best friend, June (who belongs to another friend named Steve, who loves to dance). I think it's one of Zipper's favorite times of year, too. The best part is coming home with a jar of still-warm golden-brown maple syrup to pour on my oatmeal, drizzle on pancakes, or stir into my tea.

Yours from the Puppy Place,

Ellen Miles

P.S. For another book about a puppy at a cabin in the woods, try *Kodiak*.

THE NAME GAME:

How to find the best name for your new puppy

1. What does your puppy look like? Is he a giant Great Dane (like Moose) or a tiny Yorkie mix (like Bitsy)? Is she white (like Snowball) or black (like Shadow)? Lots of excellent dog names are based on looks.

2. Does your dog remind you of one of your heroes, or a character in a book or movie that you love? Name him or her after that person: Luke, Leia, Nala, Elsa, Harry.

3. What does your dog love to do? If he likes to sniff and search things out,

you might call him Hunter. Or if he's like my dog and loves to run fast, you could call him Zipper!

4. Want to find the most popular names? You can use baby-name or puppy-name websites. Bella, Lucy, Max, and Bear are always popular choices.

5. Just remember, the best names are short—two or three syllables at most—and easy to pronounce. Some trainers believe that dogs respond best to two-syllable names with a vowel sound at the end, like Bingo or Buddy.

TOP TEN REASONS YOUR FAMILY MIGHT BE READY FOR A DOG:

10. You have a safe place to let your dog play, like a fenced yard or nearby dog park.

9. Your family is willing to spend the money necessary for food, vet bills for regular checkups, and emergencies.

8. Everyone in the family is willing to help with walking, feeding, and cleaning up after the dog.

7. Nobody in the family is allergic to dogs.

6. Your family enjoys "staycations" at home, or likes to drive to nearby places for vacation.

5. You (and your siblings if you have them) have shown that you can be responsible by doing any assigned chores and/or helping out when asked.

4. You've spent time learning about dogs and puppies and how to take care of them and train them.

3. You have researched which breed or mix of breeds would be best for your family.

2. You have helped take care of a friend's or neighbor's dog, or have helped out at an animal shelter.

And the top reason your family might be ready for a dog?

1. You all love dogs and can't wait to have one of your own!

QUIZ: HOW WELL DO YOU KNOW YOUR DOG?

(If you don't have a dog, you can picture the imaginary dog of your dreams, or take this quiz thinking of your aunt's dog, your cat, your goldfish, or your friend's iguana!)

1. Who in your family is your dog's favorite person?
2. What is your dog's favorite thing to eat?
3. What is your dog's favorite activity?
4. Where does your dog especially love to be petted?
5. What is one thing your dog is afraid of?
6. Does your dog snore when he sleeps?
7. What trick is your dog best at?
8. What is your dog's favorite smell?
9. Does your dog have a best friend, human or dog?

10. Would your dog rather be on the couch, at the beach, or at the dog park?

11. What is the one trick your dog will probably never learn?

12. What is your dog's favorite toy?

13. What does your dog do when she is excited?

14. Where is your dog's favorite place to sleep?

15. How does your dog let you know that he loves you?

TRAINING TIPS

How to train your dog to sit in seven easy steps:

1. Have a treat in your hand, something especially tasty.
2. Call your dog to you.
3. Hold the treat over his head where he can smell it, and slowly move your hand backward.
4. When he watches the moving treat, his bottom will naturally sink toward the floor. (If it doesn't, you can gently help to push his butt down.)
5. Say the words "Good dog, sit!" as that happens.
6. Praise him again and give him the treat once he is sitting.

7. Repeat this a few times. Soon he will learn what the word "sit" means.

It's always best to keep training sessions short (ten minutes or less) and fun. Don't punish your dog if he doesn't do what you want, but be sure to always reward him when he does what you want him to do. It's also smart to end on a good note, just after he has done something right.

Remember, rewards don't always have to be food. If your dog has a favorite toy or game, those can also be rewards.

CAN YOU SPEAK DOG?

Take this quiz about dog body language and find out!

1. Your dog puts her head down and her tail between her legs. You might even see her trembling. Is your dog:
    a) happy
    b) sad
    c) afraid
    d) angry

2. A dog sneezes and wags his tail. Is he:
    a) allergic
    b) getting a cold
    c) trying to get attention
    d) excited and happy

3. You see a dog at the dog park lie down, roll over, and show her belly when she meets another dog. Is she:

   a) asking for a belly rub

   b) acting bossy

   c) telling the other dog that she is friendly and no threat

   d) trying to scratch her back on the ground

4. When you try to hug your grandma's dog, he pulls away and shows the whites of his eyes. Does he:

   a) love hugs

   b) dislike hugs

   c) have to go to the bathroom

   d) think you have bad breath

5. Your dog is in the waiting room at the vet's. She is pacing around, panting, and yawning. Is she:

   a) having a great time

   b) bored

   c) nervous

   d) tired

6. Your dog puts his paws out in front of him and his butt in the air. What is he saying?

   a) Let's play!

   b) Please scratch my butt

   c) Is it dinnertime?

   d) I'm sleepy.

WHO AM I?

1. I am a gentle giant with soft brown-and-white fur, floppy ears, and a beautiful long, feathery tail. Some folks might say I drool a little. When I'm grown up, I can weigh as much as 120 pounds! I am loyal, friendly, and calm. Long ago, I was used as a rescue dog in the Alps, finding people who were lost in the snow. Now I am most often a family pet—hopefully a family with a nice big house and yard. I am way too huge to be happy living in a small apartment.

   a) Saint Bernard

   b) beagle

   c) poodle

2. I have short, shiny, silky black fur, and my brown eyes sparkle because I love everybody. I'm so friendly that I'll lick your face all over just to prove it! I'm a medium-to-large dog, so I can do a lot of really neat things like being a guide dog, bird dog hunting companion, or hiking buddy. But my favorite thing to do is to play fetch, especially in the water. I LOVE water! I am kind, loyal, energetic, and easygoing, which makes me an ideal pet for many people.

a) Chihuahua

b) Labrador retriever

c) Jack Russell terrier

3. I am mostly white with patches of black and tan. My ears stand halfway up, then flop over, and my tail is short and stubby. I can jump up and down as if my short muscular legs

were pogo sticks! I love to chase, pounce, bark, and dig, but I also like to play with toys. I may be small (I usually weigh only about ten pounds), but I am fearless and always ready for action. Since I am not used much for hunting anymore, I need to have a lot of exercise to keep me out of trouble. Then I will be a friendly and a completely devoted family member.

a) Jack Russell terrier

b) Labrador retriever

c) poodle

4. Some people call me the polka-dot dog because my short shiny fur is white with black spots all over. I may even have a black patch over my eye that makes me look like a pirate! In olden days, my job was to run alongside a fire wagon that was pulled by horses, and I still like to hang out at firehouses. I have a long head with soft ears.

I have a big, deep bark. I am strong and smart but also very sensitive and calm. Humans are my favorite companions, so don't leave me alone too long!

a) German shepherd

b) dalmatian

c) springer spaniel

5. I'm a sleek, medium-sized dog with silky black-and-white fur and a long feathered tail. Sometimes I'm known as a "sheepdog" because I can herd animals into a big pack. In fact, I love to herd people, too! I really don't like to sit around much: I am no couch potato! I am smart and love to work, and would be happiest living on a farm with animals or with people who are as energetic as I am.

a) dachshund

b) poodle

c) border collie

6. I have a thick fluffy coat with mostly black, gray, and white markings, and I love winter! My ears are triangular and erect, and my fluffy tail rolls over my back. I have either brown or light blue eyes; sometimes I may have one of each! In snowy climates, I can work with a team of other dogs to pull sleds over long distances because I have great stamina and wide paws for running on snow. I am friendly and affectionate, but I can be stubborn, too. Since I get bored easily, I like to live with people who are active outdoors.

a) Afghan hound

b) schnauzer

c) husky

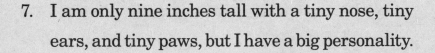

7. I am only nine inches tall with a tiny nose, tiny ears, and tiny paws, but I have a big personality.

My coat is quite beautiful—silky brown-and-black with just a touch of silver. It is definitely long enough for a pretty bow! I love to play outdoors, but I am well behaved in an apartment. Sometimes I can be stubborn, but don't let my small size fool you. Not only am I beautiful, but I am brave and make a good watchdog, too!

a) Great Dane

b) Yorkshire terrier

c) French bulldog

8. I am small and muscular with a funny flat face and sweet bulgy brown eyes. I have soft velvety ears and a curled tail. My fur is especially soft and shiny. Some people think I look worried because I have wrinkles all over my forehead, but actually I'm a real clown. I love to cuddle and play, and you can always

find me sniffing, snorting, or sneezing about something!

a) Jack Russell terrier

b) pug

c) whippet

9. I am a goofball, I admit it! I'm also very smart and friendly, and more than anything I love to be with people. I have chocolate-brown eyes, floppy ears, silky-soft golden fur, and a beautiful, feathery tail. I can be trained to do whatever you want. I can be a guide dog, a hunting dog, or just the best friend you ever had. Not to boast, but I am one of the most popular breeds of all time.

a) golden retriever

b) pug

c) whippet

10. I'm a large dog with a thick shiny coat in shades of tan, brown, and black. My ears stand straight up, and I have big brown eyes and a long sharp nose. I'm smart, alert, noble, and elegant looking (but not conceited! Really!). Some folks are scared of me, but I'm not mean unless I'm trained to be. In the old days, I tended flocks and carried messages in wartime. Now I'm used as a guide dog and therapy dog, for search and rescue, as a police dog or guard dog, or just as a family companion. I can do all those things—and more!—because I am brave, obedient, and loyal.

a) Weimaraner

b) Saint Bernard

c) German shepherd

ANSWER KEY

Can You Speak Dog?

1. c 2. d 3. c 4. b 5. c 6. a

Who Am I?

1. SAINT BERNARD (like Maggie in *Maggie and Max*)
2. LABRADOR RETRIEVER (like Shadow)
3. JACK RUSSELL TERRIER (like Rascal)
4. DALMATIAN (like Cody)
5. BORDER COLLIE (like Flash)
6. HUSKY (like Bear)
7. YORKSHIRE TERRIER (like Princess)
8. PUG (like Pugsley)
9. GOLDEN RETRIEVER (like Goldie)
10. GERMAN SHEPHERD (like Scout)